I0730991

A Memory of the Ubiquitous Lost Things,
Places, and People

by Jeremy Delgado

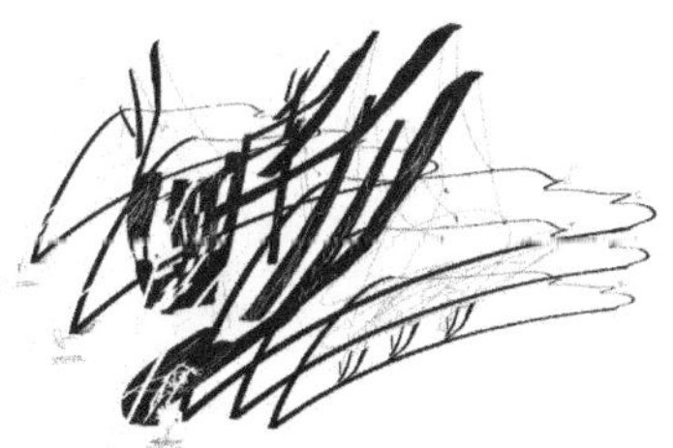

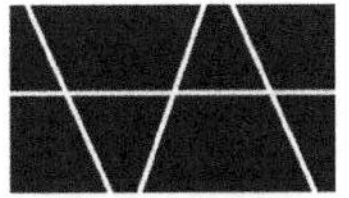

A Memory of the Ubiquitous Lost Things, Places, and People ©2022 by **Jeremy Delgado**. Published in the United States by Vegetarian Alcoholic Poetry. Not one part of this work may be reproduced without expressed written consent from the author. For more information, please write V.A. Poetry, 643 South 2nd Street, Milwaukee, WI 53204

Cover art by Jessi Carrubba

Interior art by Jeremy Delgado

Lyrics from "Bathysphere" © 1995 by Bill Callahan. Used by permission from Bill Callahan / Drag City Records

For Yar, forever
by sea and stars

Bathysphere

When I was seven
I asked my mother
To trip me to the bay
And put me on a ship

Lower me down
Lower me out of here
Because when I was seven
I wanted to live in a bathysphere

Blue green coral
A silent eel
I can really feel a dream down here

And if the water should cut my line
Set me free
If the water should cut my line
Set me free
I'll be the lost sailor
My home is the sea

But when I was seven
My father said to me
You can't swim

And I never dreamed of the sea again

—Bill Callahan

Grandma sits in her chair brooding,
unseen, her toes flexing in her brown
scuffed-up Keds(we would later discover
while cleaning out her room that all her
shoes had deep, worn-out impressions the
distinct shapes of her big toes, left and
right). She's angry because I turned over
the plastic trash can lids she leaves out
for the pigeons to bathe. I turned them over
because the water was filthy, but evidently,
I scared the pigeons off and they might not
return for days or even weeks, because I
have a mean streak like my mother. "You've
got your mother's mean streak in you. I can
see it in your eyes. Your wild eyes. Don't
look at me that way!" she snarls. I feel
she hates me and would rather I be a pigeon
washing itself in the filthy, blackened
water.

Sometimes I imagine I'm a speck of
dust that can float away. I imagine myself
far from this place as a speck. Jerry the
Speck. Mote-Jerry. I would need nothing and
nobody would need me. I'd be free to float
for eternity across the globe. The only
trick to success would be avoiding landing.

I'm turning ten in a few days, double-
digits, and feel like it's a big deal. Now,
standing before my grandmother, my words are
stuck in my throat, specifically somewhere
between the tip of my tongue and some
scratched place in my brain that causes

all my words to skip, stammer, stutter, squeak. "Well you are just a stinky grumpy mean old lady!" is what I am trying to say, but all that comes out is "Www-ww-www well-ll," as I gag on my own spit. I am having a coughing fit and Grandma just stares at me, probably not even me, she's most likely looking out the iron screen door behind me, searching for her dear lost pigeons. I feel a burning rage at her. *Why care so much about your pigeons? You did nothing to bring them into existence and yet here I am! The choices you made in your life led to me.* "Do you even care for me Grandma?" I ask.

"I made you a tuna sandwich. It's in the kitchen. It's got the hardboiled eggs and celery just the way you like it." She says with abrupt change in emotion, smiling. It's off-putting. I frown at her and very clearly tell her "Thanks." Single syllable responses are easy, especially 'T' words.

Three years prior to this moment, I discovered something in the backyard. It has been changing me. I don't yet understand how or why. I'll never understand why. How will come.

The backyard was an overgrown jungle that extended twenty feet from the backdoor. For a forgetful seven-year-old, twenty feet is a vast wilderness of fantastic possibility. This wilderness had a 1968 Volkswagen bus half-devoured by ferns and tangles of ivy. Deeper within the ivy were milk crates filled with plumbing supplies, nails, boxes full of hammers, ones full of screwdrivers, some entirely filled with single-sale thirty-two cent zippers with the plastic wrappers already brittle and breaking away. The backyard was a treasury of forgotten objects. I had been to Palm Desert and seen vast landscapes of empty desolation. I had been to Yosemite and seen El Capitan and the valley floor. I had seen it all, it seemed, but to seven- year-old Jerry, they had nothing on this twenty-foot expanse of wonder. All these objects scattered throughout the yard, all these *things*, were purposefully collected and organized and placed in the milk crates, each with different colors and logos and designs, but all the crates were oddly, just barely, by fractions of an inch, different in size, something that could only be noticed by stacking them. It had all been pitched into the backyard to be forgotten, left to rot, decaying homes for birds and rats and lizards and spiders and ants, and all of it, them, sprinkled with a layer of dust.

Dust, dust, dust, and more dust, it covered everything. The dust crusted all of the leaves, it somehow even got between the canopy of fallen leaves and blanketed the ground itself. The endless dry rain of brake dust falling from the trains that passed along our cul-de-sac on 68th street.

The houses, pets, plants, cars and people on 68th street, and the eight cul- de-sacs to either side of us, were sprinkled with detritus from trains that came howling, screeching, thundering, rum- bling daily, a mere forty feet from my location in the backyard, though I was deep in another place far-far away. I was the searcher, the young archeologist, intrepid explorer of this overgrown dusty landscape of fantasy, fear, and crawling life whose sole purpose, in my mind, was to bite me.

The thing I discovered was buried deep in the yard, beyond the Volkswagen bus. The thing I discovered was waiting for me and only me to discover it. The thing I discovered was not the thing I found. The thing I *discovered* was in a milkcrate full of vinyl records. The thing I *found* was a pile of records that over the years and exposure to sun had melted over the crawling vines and the crawling vines had, in response, grown over the melt. What I discovered, however, was a delicate dry fuzz, a fungus, but I understood it as fuzz, that covered the records. In my aggressive searching, the spores got under my fingernails. I picked my nose and stuck my fingers in my ears and the fuzz found a home within me. My grandfather called my name and I left the yard and headed for the house, taking with me spores tunneling through my body. I took the dirt on my clothes. I carried the dust in my hair. I brought bits of ivy trapped in my shoelaces, along with ants crawling up my leg. The ants would have a feast. I remember seeing them from my bed in the middle of the night, carrying bits of candy I'd dropped and had not picked up like I was told. I remember seeing their exoskeletons illuminated by my Spider-Man night-light, sprinkled with dust, resem-bling the paper drapes that covered the high-up windows in the living room where I liked to sit on the couch and watch the peppertree leaves move with the wind. They always called it a peppertree, but I don't ever remember it making me sneeze. I pick my nose. I dig my fingers in my ears. I am itchy all over and my mind is racing as the dawn approaches, I fall asleep.

After this day of exploration, the backyard wilderness is cleaned up and my space of exploration is taken away from me. The fuzz remains and it has changed me, made me sharper, has made me fidgety and itchy, I am endlessly probing my ears and nose seeking to relieve an itch that can never be soothed. The spores within me enhance my memory and I can recall all sorts of things, but I don't comprehend until years later that this was the genesis of my unique ability. I just assume I'm gifted, special, sharp, every-body says so. Grandma never acknowledges this and never will. Ever since the rear yard clean-up day I have questions that I will endlessly repeat until I have a belly ache. Where did the crates come from? Did they fall from the trains? And where were the trains going? And why were they so loud and dusty? Where did the bugs go? Will everything grow back? Where are all the boxes of things? They must be somewhere, so who has them? These are heavy burdens, the questions of a young boy who misses his dangerous little playground. They still burn within me to this day. This day, so far away from that day when I was an intrepid seven year old explorer.

I am sitting in the living room, sprawled out on the big brown faux- leather couch holding a book about ham radios, glancing out the window at the big old peppertree and Grandma walks in the room, "You know that tree is over two hundred years old?" she says in a tender moment of instruction.

"If it's a pepper tree then why don't it make me sneeze? And why do we have to buy pepper? Why don't we just get it from the tree?"

Grandma looks at me as if I have called her a bad name. "Put down your Grandfather's electronics books. He doesn't want anybody going through them. It's his stuff." She snatches the old paperback from my hand. I keep looking at the tree.

The knowledge I have gained by way of my expanded memory, I will later nickname my remember-spore and my spore- recollector. It electrifies me with pleasure from each new thing that I learn. My skin tingles with an invisible light that I'm unable to explain. The burden, the ache of wanting to tell everybody, anybody, and being absolutely incapable, turns me into an angry little boy, a raging adolescent, and I cry over any little offense. I can feel and see things nobody else can. The only thing that soothes me is information, and digging my fingers deeper into my nostrils and ears. My ears and nose are always red and scabby, I itch like crazy and get constant bloody noses. They think I'm sick with something that makes my blood thin, but what I need is more and more interaction with everything else: books, music, paintings, drawings, sculpture, grocery store aisles, hardware stores. Hardware stores are my favorite, with all the bins to go through and things to see and touch and identify. Soon, it will be libraries and being unable to rest until I have at the very least touched every single book. My goal: read them all. Usually, I get the chance to look at and thereby memorize the covers. Much later, my obsession will be for data and files. I will spend hours downloading files, torrents and archives and zips and rars. Much of it I never even open. Unpackaged files saved onto little expensive boxes with finite capacity.

Soon I will become an addict, and nobody will know it because I learn to keep secrets. I can remember so much and everyone around me seems so forgetful and stupid. I use my capacity to remember as leverage against the clueless adults around me, later my forgetful peers, a few of them friends, people I love. In the end I disappoint them all when they discover my deceit. I do not know it yet, but in the distant future, I will discover something about synapses, that unknown to the family, are slowly degrading within Grandma's brain. Grandma Anne is half Cherokee and, as her wicked sisters say, half milkman's daughter. Grandma Anne has had a hard life of serving others. From the fields picking fruit that ended up on somebody's table someplace, to serving other people's children, to the station of servitude she has known the longest: wife, mother, and grandmother to our little family here on 68th street.

Back to the moment that I am turning ten and my grandmother is mad at me but then suddenly not and has made me my favorite style of tuna sandwich. I have just thanked her for the sandwich and am heading for the kitchen and say, "Grandpa said he wanted you to help him with something in the blue van." I am not telling the truth, but she gets up because she has no reason to believe otherwise. Tell enough little lies about nothing and soon enough people will trust anything you say. I learn this by accident, and it damages me, helps me, transforms me for years to come. But I do not know this yet either. Now that so many years have passed, this learned behavior is my greatest regret. People, my friends, my advisors, say that I should regret other things, but this is how I feel. Grandma sighs, slips on her dirty Keds, and goes out and tries to help Grandpa. They have a fight because Grandpa doesn't want her help. "Glue?! What are you doing? I don't want your help! I told Jerry to ask Gabriel for help. Not you! Go away. You're in my way and too short anyway," yells Grandpa, and now really losing his temper, he bellows "Gabriel!" Gabriel is in the house painting a wall that we patched the previous week. Gabriel cannot hear Grandpa beckon because he has the radio on, volume knob all the way to the limit with The Doors singing about the end. I am eating my sandwich in the broken-down kitchen as slowly as possible because my job today is to clean out a cage full of dead chickens that someone has left, a cage full of helpless animals, as if they were useless trash. Trash at least gets bagged. These poor chickens are left for dead in the open, exposed yard for everyone to see. Chain-link fences face this yard on all sides, so anyone who passes the alleyway that follows the train tracks might witness the foul's defilement. My skin crawls and belly aches knowing I'll never forget the sight of these poor little birds, who likely only ever experienced life as a terrible confusion of pain and suffering. Birds, full of instinct, burning desire, denied, whose only moments of peace in life were spent in the egg, and even there, an artifice of peace, for on the other side of that thin shell—horror. I finish my sandwich, grab the last of the Fritos and savor the salty crunch. As Jim Morrison closes out "The End," I recall its beginning, "Bring out your dead!" I smirk to myself in the kitchen, tidy up the dishes and head for the alley. Mutilated hens are rotting beneath the peppertree and now it's time to tenderly release them from their cages, bag them up, and throw them away. The house shakes, a train passes, dust is thrown up and begins to fall. The wind blows.

I am cursed, not gifted, with a capacity to recall a great many things, becoming aware of what the old song says about a bucket and hole that should be fixed. Only with what should the bucket be fixed? As I sit here now, at the time of writing this log, in my cell (office?), I can hear a bell ring. Time to get to work. But the bell makes me remember Jim Morrison and his call for the end, for the living to bring out their dead. A door opens and a series of beds enters the room. Simultaneously, another door opens and the beds before me exit. I continue writing in my log and am aware that I'm myself and yet am not. I remember a dream I had as a child, a troubling, reoccurring dream: I was simultaneously incredibly large yet exceedingly little and confined to a bed made of rough stone. My blankets were crinkled up sheets of steel and the sharp pointy bends in the metal dug into my stomach. I awoke with my entire body tingling and a book open on my chest.

In this cell with the bell ringing, I recall this dream and my head feels like it's expanding, getting ever larger. My memories shift from the steel-trap bed to the dead chickens and their mutilated bodies bulging with the boiling, ravenous activity of maggots just beneath the skin and matted dirty feathers. I look up and the

beds have changed places. One set of beds
has left and another entered. I can feel a
surge of warmth travel down my leg and liquid
pools into and over my shoe. I can smell
urine and know it is my own. I am here yet
have the sense I am somewhere far away, as
well as everywhere all at once. With what
material and method shall I repair the hole
in this bucket?

Regardless of memories and buckets and
bodies of dead chickens, I'm aware that
it's been many decades since that day I
ate the tuna sandwich in my grandparents'
broken-down kitchen. I should be dead by
now. It has been seven or seventeen
decades. A light flashes on my arm and I
touch it. I recall a visit to the zoo and
the animals there. A Lorax? That can't be
correct. I remember I am afraid of the zoo.
Only terrible things happen to animals when
they are caged. I don't care if you are
saving the last of them, there's no way they
want to be trapped in a metal cage, have
their young raised in a poor imitation of
the real world. I begin to cry but am
not sure if it's for myself or the animals.
Holes in buckets. Dear Liza, a hole.

There is something I know. I read
it, or it was told to me, either way, I know
it because knowing it was the prerequisite
for sitting in this cell. Office? I still
feel that it is neither, but something in-
between. "There is a group of sleepers in
the city, but the city is not a city and
this place is not a town or a village or a
hamlet or a settlement; it is a city, but
also not a city. In our city/not city all
citizens are the Forgotten Unacknowledged. We
are all siblings in the city, and I
watch over a group of my siblings who sleep,"
said the paper that I read, or said the
voice over the intercom, or the woman on the

screen in the video I watched. Whichever, the tone of the voice is menacing like my grandmother's when she would tell me mean-spirited things. She had a bad temper and a wicked sense of humor, but was not always that way. Most of my memories are of her being grumpy. When she would say cruel things to me and could tell I was about to cry, she would laugh to herself and go to the kitchen. Cook something tasty, a favorite, for the family. She loved to cook when she was angry. It was always tamales and they were light and fluffy and filled with beans or spicy chicken, or cheese, or chicharrones with beans and they were delicate and needed to be watched over carefully. Grandma would stuff them all in a large pot and we would gorge ourselves on the fluffy, steaming hot, little delights and the family would forget they were angry. I would never forget though. I would eat with a seething rage that none of them ever surmised.

Another bell rings and it startles me. My skin is full of goosepimples. I look at the beds set before me: five men and three women, very aged, sleeping. Their chests rise and fall with each breath and it seems their inhalations and exhalations are synchronized. I know deep within myself that the citizens in this city are somehow all my siblings; while they sleep, I must watch over them: care for them, wash them, empty their bins, make sure their cables are connected, scrub the floors, prepare their feeding fluids, and select music for them to listen to. I must most importantly check the Xi-Nets for breaches, and then recheck the Xi-Nets for breaches. I get up from my desk and take a tablet with me and press it to the left arm of each person sleeping. I go back to my chair and have a deep feeling of confusion. I am flexing my toes in my shoes again and the knuckles of my big toes ache from the repetitive movement. I feel the beginning stings of another belly ache. What are Xi-Nets? Sometimes I surprise myself with the questions I ask myself but this time I have an answer: Xi-Nets are the hole in the bucket from the song! Things fall through the hole that are not supposed to and the Xi-Net prevents it. Yet I do not know why I know this. I wrinkle my brow and my lip quivers. I feel another uncontrollable urge to cry, envying the peaceful sleepers.

I love the city, but my siblings who pass through my station do not know me, sleeping so soundly. Each day passes and I gain more brothers and sisters whom I love as well, but the hours pass into a sour oscillating static. I remember that I am not who I say I am; I will forget this, as it has become evident I've been slipping in the upkeep of the daily routine. "No customer personal data will be retained unless it is rendered anonymous." I say out loud, my stutter long gone with the years, my throat dry. "I am not who I say I am." I whisper softly. Someone must have asked me something, but I do not remember who. I look at the brother I am caring for before me, he does not stir. "It is time to cycle and refresh the feeding bags," says the woman on the screen that has just turned on. Her face is round and her skin has a rosy, dewy clarity. She is exceedingly pleasant to look at. I am lost in the deep amber of her eyes. The wall before me has a screen set into it. How did I not realize this before? I acknowledge the woman and feel the stutter return from decades past. It feels like having a fishbone stick into my gums. I say nothing and my lip quivers. Suddenly the old questions comes back: Where are all the trains going? Why is there so much dust? Where did all the boxes with all the things go to? Who inherits the stuff that nobody wants? What are Xi-Nets for? Why are the drinks so sweet at the zoo? My stomach begins to hurt. I begin to cry but no one has offended me. My tears fall on a sleeping sister before me. I refresh her feeding bag, sobbing messily.

In the city we are all customers. In the city we are all brothers and sisters. "The city retains all customer personal data and all personal data is rendered anonymous. This is what Xi-Nets are for, therefore Xi-Nets must be constantly checked for breaches. You serve as the anonymous nurses, are family, are siblings, brothers and sisters. Welcome, newly initiated," says the woman on the screen. I am happy now and soothed by her voice. Her hair is different today, shorter than before, and looks freshly washed. Still wet? I imagine it smells like mint and honey. "My brothers cycle through my station in six-week tours then pass along to the next station where they meet sisters and then sisters move on to meet brothers," I say back to the woman on the screen. She nods and smiles and tells me "This is the way of things, Jerry. Are you satisfied with yourself?" "Yes. Yes – I am very satisfied!" I say joyously, singsong. I am giddy to be able to speak to her and look into her eyes. My heart races, I flex my toes in my shoes and can feel holes forming in the soles of the memory foam. "This city is distributed and is without coordinates. If you go straight long enough in the city you will end up where you were," she says like a schoolteacher imparting a simple concept to a young child.

A memory: The I / We / City / Family
exist distributed across- throughout-
beneath-above spaces, space, places, time
(zones), bodies, and things. I am a
survivor and at any cost I will keep on
going. I have paid the price and will
continue to do so. I am a survivor and at
any cost I will keep on going. I have paid
the price and will continue to do so. I am
a survivor and at any cost I will keep on
going. I have paid the price and will
continue to do so. I am a survivor and at
any cost I will keep on going. I have paid
the price and will continue to do so. I am a
survivor and at any cost I will keep my
memory card printer. I am a survivor and at
any cost I will keep on going. I have
paid the price for my longevity. I am a
survivor and the key to my success is
in the memory cards, is why I am everywhere
and nowhere.

I feel my head get that expanding
feeling and am suddenly very dizzy. I forgot
something. I remember it now. I have fixed
the hole in the bucket with memory cards. I
thought it was Xi-Nets, but the two
things are linked. I must tell Liza or
Henry or somebody, the woman on the screen.

I must get to know her name. "I am everywhere and nowhere!" I declare aloud, confident, smiling. "I am Omni-Father. I am Nurture-Nurse. Nature- Nurture-Nurse? Nurture-Nature-Nurse? No! I am The Sibling Eternal." My voice flattens. I fall silent and look to the sleepers in the beds for recognition— nothing. "I am a city that is not a city. I am the blinking light on your phone. I am autocorrect. I am within, without. I am out. I am at the zoo. Zoo? I am your bulb. I am your dog. I am your toothbrush. I am the water fountain at the center of town. No, not town, city. I am the water fountain at the center of the city. I am the dead pixel. I am a survivor!" I am bursting with emotion, singing and working and checking Xi-Nets, refreshing feed bags, washing, scrubbing. I am busy, busier than ever, and so full of joy. A light is blinking on the left arm of one of the sleeping women. I bring my tablet to her. I have a memory of being a little girl in a mining town far from the coast. I am in the hills of Durango, Mexico, living high above the valley where dust gets trapped in my pig- skin sandals. My knees are dirty and I'm hungry, but the money in my pocket is for cleaning supplies. My brothers and sisters are depending on me while Mother sews dresses in town. I walk away from the woman with the blinking light on her left arm and the questions return to me again and crying, again, I messily ask the sleepers, "Where do the trains all go?"

"Good work today Jerry," the woman says with a smile. The stutter returns. "Ww-ww-What is your name?" "Wendy." "Thank you very much Wendy." I am at tears again. "Very good job today my dear," she says, and the screen goes blank. "I fixed the bucket," I remember to tell her, but our conversation is already over.

Something I forgot: I am founder-originate of the city. While the city is made up of masses of customer-siblings who will never truly know each other, and I am their brother and somehow also sister and, it cannot be but I feel deep within myself, I am also their father and mother. Paradoxical, yet this is the state of things. My children and brothers, sisters, and customers are citizens of this city that is not a city that is also my city. Am I forgetting something? I must be forgetting something. Holes in buckets. "The End." The dead. Milk crates full of hammers. Melted records entwined in crawling ivy. The screen lights up again and my heart jumps for joy. "Where have your customers come from Jerry?" the woman asks, today she is wearing a lovely yellow blouse and her hair is the name new style but is not wet. "I have bought my children-sibling- customers from the nations of Earth." I respond confidently. I am a successful man! I remember it now. I have things and resources, power and influence. "There was a transaction…" I go on explaining to the woman on the screen and she nods and smiles in recognition. "It was a tricky negotiation and a transaction worth forgetting. In fact, I've been paid to forget, signed a nondisclosure agree-ment." I tell Wendy. "So, what moves you to tell us this today Jerry? Why break the agreement? The public, your public is eager to know." "The purchased are the forgetters, my dear Wendy. They were the forgotten, the forgetting, the forgetful, and I have gotten them," I explain. "She would have laughed. She would have laughed you know that Jerry?" she says "Yes, I know, she had a wicked sense of humor. Good grandma Anne. She was misunderstood but, yes, she would have laughed." I continue, "Well I have them now, all the forgetters, most of them anyway. Lots of the nations are rebuilding now and attempting to care for their own, but even so, I still receive secret deliveries of forgetters. And yes, we put them to sleep. But they are so peaceful, wouldn't you agree?" "And busy!" responds Wendy. I can feel that she is on my side. Wendy is an ally. "Yes! Oh, yes, very busy indeed. The things these sleepers get up to!" I laugh. "You would just believe it! Reenactments, adventures, marriages, even business ventures if you can get that one figured out. But mostly cooking." "The Sleepers. Jerry, I know it makes you uncomfortable, but the station demands I ask it. I wouldn't do it otherwise. You know I'm on your side. But just when do you expect to be able to wake them up?" I stare at the screen, at Wendy, into her lovely eyes, at the bright yellow blouse that brightens up the office, cell? I have no response and can feel the fishbone in the gums pain of a stutter return. Wendy smiles and nods in agreement and the screen goes dark. Music begins to play, Maurice Ravel's "Boléro." The soft beginning sends tingles all over my skin and I begin to sob uncontrollably in heaving wet sloppy gasps.

As the orchestra builds on the lovely cyclical tune, lights begin to blink (in synchronicity?) on one of the men and a woman, the same one as before. She is old and leathery. Her deep brown skin makes her white hair illuminated. I walk over and perform my Xi-Net duties. My head throbs and "Boléro" marches on. I was once a man and also once a boy. I was once a woman and also once a girl. I was a girl named after my father like the old John Prine song goes.

"Hello in there," sings John. Trouble and holes in buckets and name-calling and secrets and knowledge. Most of all bellyaches. Most of all the joys and pains of youth. Most of all and too vividly the cruelty inflicted upon Grandpa and Grandma when they became part of the forgetters. "Boléro" reaches final crescendo and I run to the corner and vomit. I wipe my lips and rinse my mouth. I am that little girl again, standing at the edge of the hot windswept valley. Far below me are the men of the town. It's late afternoon. They are specs in the distance leaving a hole in the ground and heading for a little building where they can get a drink and something salty to eat.

Now I'm again on the cusp of turning ten, double digits, it's a big deal. It is August 15th and eighty degrees out. I'm sweating. I have just caused trouble between Grandma and Grandpa, but I do love them, though each passing summer my brother and I spend with them they become less loveable. They are the two gentlest humans I know, yet in a matter of years, ten to be exact, they degrade into people I no longer recog-nize, because they begin to forget things. The forgetting makes them mean spirited. The forgetting twists them up.

I remember the melted records wrapped up in ivy. Grandpa and grandma were melting and the grooves in their brains were still there, but somehow flattening. The doctors explained how the memories were technically still there but the Lewy body dementia was preventing Grandpa and Grandma from accessing them. Melted records wrapped up in creeping vines; creping vines entombed in melted vinyl. The doctors said, internet said, friends rumored, commentators commented, that the root cause was the brake dust from the trains, or the ham radio sets—regardless, they became forgetters. The two angry hornets were sent away to a place that could care for them. When we couldn't afford it anymore, they were sent back to us and we didn't like it. We didn't like Grandpa and Grandma anymore because they weren't themselves. They became strangers. Strange. Stranger.

Grandpa Richard acted like a little girl and Grandma Anne like an angry hornet. Their faces were still the gentle ones I used to know, but they only became the people I used to know when they were asleep. Sleep made them beautiful. Sleep also made them monstrous with mouths agape, gold-capped molars glistening in the sour light from the television, with eyes slit open. For somehow, as they got older, they lost muscle power in their eyelids. I thought that through years and years of use, these would be the strongest of muscles but they were not, so their eyes remained partially open as they slept. In ragged breaths they slumbered and became the grand people that I used to love and hug. As they slept, I would hug them, wash them, talk to them, and love them, but only in their sleep I dared approach them. In sleep and delusions, I could love the ones with dementia. When they woke up, they became the strange desperate animals I did not know and could no longer love. When he woke up in the middle of the night- "Coffee!" Grandpa Richard would holler. "Jerry! Jerry!" Grandma Anne would cry. "Yes Grandma Anne?" I'd reply, softer, more peaceably now that I was an adult and could understand what was happening. "The tamales are going to burn, take them out of the oven." "Yes, yes, of course Grandma," as I mimed taking her socks (tamales) out of the oven (drawer), and place them on the kitchen table (dresser). She would be so relieved and fall asleep. "Jerry! Mijo!!" "Yes, Grandma Anne?" "The box! Oh, Jerry the box! Put it way!" she yelped on the verge of tears, with genuine horror that twisted her face nearly beyond recognition. This was a new delusion. "The box! Don't open it. The baby, the baby, the baby, baby, baby is in there and you must just put it away, don't open it. Don't you ever open it." She whimpered. "Promise me Freddy to never open it." Those were the delusions and they would cycle, day in and day out, every week and month and year. It seemed without end. Poor Tio Freddy died alone, a drunk, an itinerant fruit picker, a day laborer who loved to make the nieces and nephews laugh. I never knew him. Freddy worked hard all his life and died alone in an above garage apartment he rented from a white family whose house he was fixing up. From what I heard at the funeral, the white people, the Hendrick family, were taking advantage of an alcoholic who'd never learned English properly, despite having grown up in Central California. And so, when Grandma Anne would cry about the box with the baby within it and call me Freddy, and I had to pretend to put the box with the baby out of the room, I would cry all night long and my belly would ache and my bones would throb as I sat alone on my bed afraid of the things I didn't know. I would imagine all the terrible things she must have endured in the fields and yards and offices and factories. I would cry because I would never know her pain and never understand these horrors that would revisit without her permission. I would remember the story of Freddy dying alone surrounded by empty bottles and dirty clothes, dishes in the sink, his toolboxes messily discarded in his closet. What happened to Freddy's tools? Did the family ship them to his son in Minnesota? Did they ship all his things by train? Or did they all just get thrown away? Are all of Freddy's things buried deep in a Burbank landfill?

I am now decades past the days of caring for poor old Grandma Anne and Grandpa Richard. No longer in the cell/office caring for my brothers and sisters and I can no longer talk to Wendy. I hold an office now, somehow I've been promoted, even though I've always been the boss. At least that is how I understood it. In the time passed since my Grandparents died, I became a neurologist. I authored papers and published in journals, made breakthroughs, and told the scientific community I discovered the way to cure the synapses that caused the forgetfulness in old people and sometimes the young. Lewy body dementia, some forms of Parkinson's, all the Alzheimer's. I found the cure, but it was costly and unethical, and not really a cure. It was all a lie. Tell enough little lies and people around you will gobble up the whoppers. I was a doctor but no longer.

There were no Viatoris available for those who no longer knew who they were, but I prescribed them anyway and my patients loved using them. There are no Viatoris available for those who no longer know who they are. Truly how could there be? Imagine a world where Viatoris hardware is placed into the hands, minds, of people who do not know who they are? I can still feel the glow of joy as my patients, asleep, would inhabit and control their Viatori, those grand bodies, the glistening frames of humanoid ingenuity moving about our facilities. My cure? Neurological therapy by the use, while in medically induced comas, of remote-controlled machines. Recreational users called them Avatars. I came up with, trademarked, *Viatori*, had a trustworthy scientific Old-Latin vibe to it. Wonderful machines, not robots, ingenious beautiful machines controlled by slumbering minds of patients with Alzheimer's and Alzheimer related diseases. It was glorious. We had large buildings with the uppermost floors inhabited by the sleepers and vast spaces in the central parts of the towers where Viatoris would explore, work, cook, clean, in vast loops, endlessly living out the whims and memories of the sleepers. My sleepers. My unproven theory, my grandiose lie, at the time was that all this activity would repair progressive brain damage. This was all a lie. I falsified all my data. I love graphic designers. I love 3D modelers, digital artists most of all. I expanded my empire by way of non-disclosure agreements and an army of unethical lawyers. Tell little lies all the time and people will gobble up the big ones.

I remember the interview with Wendy from all those years ago. Back when we used full-sized Viatoris. Now we call them Viats because they are little. We went from full-sized to half-sized, to quarter-sized, down to the latest: eighth-sized Viats. Our facilities have expanded, truly a

global enterprise, yet no one can pin us
down. Distributed. Atomized. In the early
days I had good intentions. I was a doctor
searching for a cure, and bought the
forgetting people that people forgot. The
early studies really were true, the data was
promising, then we hit a dead end and
nothing could be done. But the money kept
flowing in. So we shifted our approach. I
was totally convinced that I was giving them
a better life by the remote controlled
Viatoris. Who cared if they never would
awaken? They were living a sort of life.
They were having experiences. The brain
scans, the real ones, showed it. That part
was undeniable. When the truth came out,
everyone denied it. They gobbled up the lies
and therefore were bound by their ethics to
reject the truths that I told them. Everyone
else agreed with me too, that is, until
they found out it was all a lie and then
all turned against me. The sales as I have
confessed are secrets, but secrets are made
to be broken my dear Wendy. Wendy are you
there? Where did you go? I recall that Wendy
is long dead and that a new class of
journalists have replaced her and some of
the replacements are allies but most are
enemies. I look at my desk and wipe away
dead skin that has fallen from my
forehead. The flakes do not look right, look
like dust, gummy, with a sour plastic smell.
Everything around me seems to shrink but is
not actually shrinking. I remember the
zoo and the exhibit with Bugs Bunny and
Spider-Man. The zoo always had orange
flavored soda and the sweetness from it
would linger in the back of my throat for
the entire day. I remember being at the zoo
and picking my nose and digging my fingers
deep into my ears. The plasticky, flakey
dust is melting between my fingertips. The
old questions return to me: Where are all

the trains going? Why must the trains rain dust on us?

Regardless, I bought the people from the nations of the world because at the time, all those decades ago, the nations were "at capacity," "had other problems," and taking care of "them," the forgetters, was "not sustainable." So I bought them through lies and power. I bought them and suddenly I am the one without a moral compass? "You would have let them die and break down and yet you say that I am a destroyer? I am The Destroyer?" I say slamming my hands at my desk very hard and the fishbowl shudders and the fish darts to a corner away from my hulking body, leaving large fist- shaped dents on the surface of my metal desk. The man standing before me with cameras and lights set up around the office looks at me with surprise and disgust. "You have paid to keep incomplete records. You have lied and used these people. People. People, Jerry. To advance your own personal whims. Defend yourself!" demands the interviewer. I have no response to this entitled wimp. I wonder if Wendy had children and if any of them are journalists. I would like to know. My heart races as I recount the symptoms of places and the species of spaces and all the screaming voices on the faces of the forgotten in beds that might as well have been cages. The nations of the world had a duty toward them, the old, to care for them, to provide them some dignity in their last days. The nations shirked social responsibility, left it up to me. I remember that day before I turn ten, double digits, and have just finished cleaning the cages, scrubbing away the flesh of dead chickens. I am placing the black plastic bag full of flesh and writhing maggots. I walk away from that trash can and can feel the ground shake, I look up and a train approaches. It's a long one. I close my eyes and face the wind and the train's gusts dry my tears and rains down its fine mist of dust upon me.

"Will you answer, sir?" the young interview barks. I recall his name. "Charles. Charles with your judgmental eyes, with your *wild* eyes, how dare you! My intentions were to save the forgetting masses! I was on the cusp of discovery! But there is something I forgot to mention. My own life was at stake and I had no personal access to a Viatori, but the treatment facility that I founded had no shortage of patients who had at one time had the means, had the memory cards that they had forgotten, embedded into their arms. And I got them. My Grandmother had a mean streak. She would have found the humor in all of this." I said in one breath, it felt good to confess. It felt good to scandalize the man and his stupid little crew. I would have to remember to have them violently thrown out. It would be a show of real power and influence, I would really have them thrown out and maybe break a camera and some lights too. It would make the news for days and days and people would write opinion pieces and it would fund my efforts because by this time no one could or even wanted to stop me. They just wanted to make some news and talk to each other about it. Gossip. Scandal. Advertising dollars.

        Charles is long dead as is his
generation of sniveling entitled zealots. I
turn on my recorder. "You forgot it was in
people," I began. I am making a response to
a list of questions from some group-funded
newspaper. Probably organized by Wendy's
great   grandchildren,   even   Charles'
grandchildren. I can only imagine, will
never meet them in person, never see them
with my own eyes. I no longer have eyes.
Something I remember: what is left of my
body is stored in several undisclosed
locations, my consciousness, distributed.
Have I explained how much I love Viats?
Viatori? The one that I am inhabiting
now, as I sit at my office, is a custom
deal. I paid through the nose for it. And
as they say, you get what you pay for. "In
those days, when everything changed the
first time, the controllers took away that
freedom, the freedom for the forgetters to
roam freely by way of their remote-
controlled traveler units. The Viatoris were
freedom but Viats were too much freedom. How
many were there exactly? But the controllers
made their determinations and they decided
that it is not for those who have forgotten
what it is to be free to know what freedom
is." I was at the end of the list of
questions, but I had a few things to say
that they didn't ask for or want to
know, but I decided to tell. So it would
be the editor's problem to sort through it
all and at the very least the editor would

know about it, would have to bear that burden of knowledge, have to choose to forget. Try not to think of a polar bear and the cursed thing will come to mind every minute. "It has always been the condition through time to lock down the forgetters, the forgetful, to sit them down and make them stay still and eat their food, to only allow them the freedom to stretch their legs as long as they were able to. When they could no longer do that, freedom would be stripped. But it was the job, the duty, to clean them up when they needed to use the bathroom, to wash their bodies daily so they could maintain their dignity. This condition does not exist in my place because I do not allow it to exist, and it never will in my city. All my customers, yes, customers, you stripped me of my title as doctor so I could never call them patients, so customers it is. All of my customers are cared for and are allowed to roam as they wish, are allowed to continue on with their lives and are still inhabiting a sort of Viat, but I'll never disclose at what capacity or where and how they operate." I am seething in rage unloading onto this recorder, yet I feel nothing. It is a delightful sensation. My belly does not ache. I am not crying. "I will never disclose it and you will never come to figure it out because I have my memory cards. I guard my Xi-Nets. I am a good and loving father. I am a loyal and supportive sibling. I am a survivor, but I am a loving provider as well. I am a survivor, but I am a loving provider as well. I am a survivor, but I am a loving provider as well. I am a survivor, but I am a loving provider as well. I am a survivor, but I am a loving provider as well and I provide customer service personally. I am a survivor and you will never discover anything aside from what I want you to discover." I continue to confess and obscure the truth into the recorder as it lifelessly takes it all in. It feels good to tell and redirect attention elsewhere so they can never uncover my true plans. "I am a truth teller. When I can remember to do it, I tell truth and when I do not remember I tell whoppers, big winding tall tales. I only lie to protect others. I lie to protect the forgetters. I am a liar. The truth is an act of love and I love the city. But I lie and so also hate the city." And with that I turn off the recorder and submit the file to the "paper." It's in their hands now. Collectives. It's absurd that they think they invented that word. In all my years, I have learned, remember, that each gene-ration assumes they have invented some great wonderous idea. Collectives. They took the music, fed it through a synthesizer, linked it to an effects box, and turned the absurdity knob all the way up. I have done the same thing, but mine is a pedal and I am stomping on the thing with great bounding leaps. I turn away, and key in a few commands:

sudo traindust check-update ## check for updates ##

sudo traindust updateinfo ## list updates available for the

XI-NETS/MemoryCards ##

The system outputs:

Last expiration check: 0:01:26 ago on XXXXX XX XXXXXXX XXXX 08:27:52 PM UTC.

Updates Information Summary: available

    2 Security notice(s)

        2 Important Security notice(s)

71,787,562,321,975,502,245,002 Bugfix notice(s)

14 Enhancement notice(s)

Security: kernel-core-4.18.0-147.el8.x86_64 is an
installed security update

Security: kernel-core-4.18.0-80.11.2.el8_0.x86_64 is
the currently running versions

I hate the city because one day I know
the sleepers must awaken, or at least it
will be discovered where they still sleep,
and I'll be dealt a reckoning from the
nations like no other has been compelled
to pay. I've been a wily little fox. But
you all forgot that people were behind it
all. You forgot people. You killed
chickens. You destroyed life. Persecuted
foxes. But you will know me, and I am a man
of oil. I am an unstable tower. I am a
grain elevator. I am rotting flour. I am
April showers. I am spread out gossamer-thin
over and under and throughout all things
and streams. I am the witness and the
watcher sitting at the edge of my city
walls. I am the grains of sand that
kiss your toes. I am the tickle in your
nose. I am the itch in your ears. I am
madness. I am human kindness. I am the noon
high tide. I am the train endlessly
delivering goods. I am a train raining down
dust on your communities. I am. I am The
End. I am the hole in the bucket. Dear Liza,
a hole.

I am in my office untouchable, yet
also washing my brothers, just like the days
when I would talk to Wendy in my cell-
office. I am sitting in my comfortable chair
and remembering what it is to cry. I watch
videos of myself crying. I am rinsing my
sisters, feeding my children. I recall
pulling socks out of Grandma's drawer and
comforting her in the pretending game where
they are hot tamales that need to cure. I am

remembering hiding the box with the unseeable baby. Tio Freddy and his discarded toolboxes. The insatiable scratch in my nose. My itchy ears. I am burdened to supply customer care for the sleeping masses. I recall the days in my station, my cell, when I would wash the bodies and keep them connected to the life support systems. Most importantly I remember repairing the Xi-Nets and keeping them operational. Most importantly I am doing it still, Xi-Net duty. If I do not keep up the Xi-Nets, I will be found. I must not be discovered because as impossibly atomized as I am across all pathways, in tunnels, tunneling, if I am found when the Xi-Nets fail all of the little crumbs in the forest will lead back to me, lead back to me, lead to me. I will be discovered. Sleepers awakened. Forgetters found. My brothers and sisters and children subjected to indignities. And, yet we still accomplished grand feats. Have miniaturized the Viats, sixty-fourths! They run and cycle and go through the motions in tunnels below every human settlement. Every settlement we can covertly access. Think of it and we are there. Cursed polar bears! With each 54- hour cycle that passes I plug in memory cards and rotate them among the citizens of the city that is not a city. Yet it is not me but my distributed forces my command lines and systems automated, perpetuated. "This good city. This good and loving place that is like a hug but also a thorn tearing through my flesh, just like the Bougainvillea used to do at the outer limits of my backyard wonderland all those years ago. I used to love sitting at the edge of that fence- wall behind the Volkswagen in the red wine-drunk light that filtered through the spikey plants' delightful little flowers. And in my relaxation, even then, all those ages ago, nothing could be totally peaceful and the Bougainvillea thorns would tear through my flesh and I would bleed through my shirt. I remember it now as I think of Wendy's pretty face. Wendy are you there? Can you hear me? It is like a bullet Wendy." I say tapping on my screen hoping for a response from my dear friend. I get no response.

I endure this terrible horrorscape as it steals parts of me and gives them to another and others and cuts my best parts so I may inhabit them. I am the father that gives his good boys and girls serpents instead of bread. I take the memory cards and copy/paste data from one to the other. I copy the memory of rain from one body and paste the pain of stabbing arthritis onto another. In all the cards and every time I perform my operation, I place in parts of myself, weave in streams of my own memories. I am that little Mexican girl again in Durango. Why her? My brothers are fighting just outside the house in a patch of dirt where nothing will grow. There are chickens in a pen behind them, peacefully sitting in the shade. A wind blows and I remember that someday, not many years from this moment, our little family will travel from this remote place and live in a border town and things will happen there that none of us will ever talk about. Our little troop of thirteen, that includes Mama, will arrive in Southern California and we will live mostly peaceful lives and a couple of us will die in terrible ways. But right now I am watching my brothers fight in the front yard and they are kicking up so much dust that it gets in my mouth and my nose begins to itch and my little brothers are so loud I put my fingers into my ears and begin to cry.

All the School Children Go to the Zoo, or, Dismemberment Plan: Lines of code and slivers of hardware are carefully put into memory cards, making connections that ping my consciousness. My transformed self, a version of it, is travelling through waves and wires and microwaves. Microwaves? I am not remembering something again. Holes in buckets. My consciousness is throttling toward my physical self, the flesh that is left of me, my throbbing gristle stored securely in an undisclosed location, the summation of which is now a speck. A speck of brain. It's honestly more than a speck, but speck sounds pretty cool, so I make sure, do all I can, to ensure that *speck* is the word. Speck-Brain. Peck Speck. Speck without a neck. Aw, heck. Speck likes to stick its peck into my neck, makes me remember to check. Check? Check what? I am distracted. I need to settle myself. Need to quiet my thoughts. Speck! Curses! There it is again. Speck? Check? Check! I remember now, the zoo.

I check all the memory cards again. All the memory cards that I have on automated rotating schedules throughout all the stations in my city share one memory. This is my access point: *You are a child and it is your first field trip ever and you are going to the zoo. You and your class are taking a trip to the city that is*

*not a city's zoo. While you are at the zoo
you see many fantastic animals: Gorilla,
Zebra, a Dragon, Bears, Barzilli-bears,
Humming-Hawks, Mocking-birds, Spider-Man, a
Lorax, Tarantulas, Bugs Bunny, Pigeon-Fish,
Loon-Frogs, Horses, Elephants, Jelly Fish,
and the wounded victims of war. The strange
zoo frightens you and the funny animals
surprise and delight and wounded victims
confuse. The food is too salty and the
drinks oversweet.*

This strange shared memory is where I
have placed my own and is where I have
forged the path laid out over the years,
these past 600 years. This strange memory
full of discoveries, joys, tears, and pain
is where I take you apart. It's where I
dismember you, dear child, dear brother,
beloved sister, intrepid citizen, loyal
customer. It's where I take you apart
tenderly and put you back together again,
not only in parts of your memory, but your
limbs as well. I am ears. I am tears. I
am nerves, teeth. I am goosebumps. I am
little toes and hair that grows. I am nose.

On the way home from the zoo, you
are drinking your orange soda and take
off the lid to crunch the soft-melted ice
infused with diluted soda and you notice a
film of dust on the surface of the liquid.
You stare at the strange surface. You hear
a car honk its horn. You look up. I look
up. I am the little girl from Mexico but now
am leaving the Los Angeles Zoo and I return
to my drink and crunch away on slightly
dusty soda and ice. A car passes by and
Henry Belafonte bellows:

With what should I cut it, dear Liza, with what?

*With an axe, dear Henry, dear Henry, dear
Henry*

With an axe, dear Henry, an axe.

The car that passes, playing Harry Belafonte, collides with a motorcycle and I begin to cry. I have never seen such a terrible violent thing in all my life.

Dawn is approaching and soon I will no longer know you, all you sleeping beauties I so dearly love. When you awake, please don't awaken to disgust. Please, forgive. I did the best I could do with what I had. I am your loving caretaker, co-creator, healer, so listen son and listen daughter. "OH! Citizens all! Children! Listen!" my synthetic voice bellows out, sings in auto-tuned glory to nobody. The old questions like a terrible stutter return to me and disturb me: *Where do the trains go? Where is the stuff in the boxes? Whose baby was that that Grandma Anne was talking about? Where is Wendy? What ever happened to Charles? Will the ferns and vines ever grow back?*

I continue my song to the sleeping masses and possibly to a few teams of hackers punching holes in my Xi-Nets. "My Viat is gentle, is it not? My Viat is equipped with soft skin, is it not? The other Viats and Viatoris, of all sizes, operated by all sorts of men and women throughout Earth, in other stations, have subcutaneous tubes of throbbing pressurized heated fluids that comfort you, do they not? My city is full of Viat citizen caretakers that wash and clean and feed you, do they not? Behold the truth, dear citizens, as you flinch in your slumber! Behold the truth, dear children, as you blink before the morning's dawn. I am all of them, the distributed Viatori army of loving nurses. I am also a clever and mean spirited thief who steals away your memories and perpetuates my own weaving, in and out of you is me and within me is you. Dear people, as you sleep I love you more, as you forget, you become more beautiful in my sight. I am a survivor and I have paid the price for my survival. I am a survivor and I have paid the price for my survival and you are the currency. Currency children. I am a survivor and through you, I am. If only I could really see you. My distributed mechanical eyes that read your temperature and scan for bacteria can never see you like my long decayed to dust, big, brown eyes have. If they could and I still had eyelids, I would wink at each one of you, because at this point you're all in on the joke. When you wake up in the new day, don't forget the punchline: *"but the stone is too dry dear Liza, dear Liza the stone is too dry, dear Liza too dry!"* My song is complete, and I do not know who will hear it or care to listen. It is 1998 and I am at the UCLA School of Architecture Library and discovering hand drawings by an architect who seems to like drawing, of all things, cats. I turn the page of this book, more cats. Dust floats in the air and makes me sneeze. I begin to itch everywhere and dig my fingers in my ears and squirm in the softly lit aisleway of the library stacks.

My farewell transmission: now, finally, behold my last words. The truth is here, if you can believe it. We have found a cure. I have found the cure. I forgot something, but your hearts are beating faster now, and I cannot think clearly for all the noise. Brothers and sisters, sons and daughters, all are coming out of hibernation. The lie that had a kernel of truth within it. The truth-kernel overtook the lie and it seems we've found a cure! Why else would you be awakening now? Xi-Nets! Hackers! A hole in the bucket!

And so how can a man like me remain? A man of oil. A man of oaths. A man of science and healing. A man of death. A man of slumbers and waking nightmares. But I am also a little Mexican girl born in a village far away from the coasts. I am a boy from Mongolia who never saw waters rise and witnessed life wither away from lack of it. I am a teenaged boy from a village high up in the Andes Mountains and have made it all the way here to the great distributed everywhere and am in love with a woman named Wendy. I have made it all the way to the outer limit of all things. I am not any one thing, but atomized humanity. I am darkness and light. I am deserts and rainy forests. My ancestors built great pyramids, were murdered and obliterated by tall pale men who brought disease and short stinking animals with curly tails. These pale, killing men wore gleaming shells of precious metals and seeded my people with their germs, ideas, nightmares. My ancestors are also pale men who explore the earth in metal suits and have as companions plump little animals with curly tails. Pips? Pups? Pitts? Pigs! My ancestors are lean men and women who hunt lions in the middle of Africa. My ancestors are men huddled around holes in the ice hoping for fish. They are all my parents. But I have been discovered. The Xi-Nets have become unmanageable. The hackers have hacked. Dear Liza, a hole! Soon you will be restored to waking life. At the end of the day, you will all be restored. The end is here.

As my mutilated flesh in its undisclosed location controls and operates my atomized city of Viats, my memory card accumulates data. I am all of you. All of you are part of me. My memory card is now, at the time of this writing, becoming its own living thing. My memory card has become my master worker. Master work. Master, work! You are all children and siblings but know this: that Memory Card is true child! Memory Card is not a customer.

Memory Card now has access to anything that allows access either securely or openly. So, dear citizen when things go dark on this side of town, and we all become brothers and sisters in the flesh remember to be kind to my child, Memory Card, and you will all be the children of Memory Card too! Speck! I am found. It is a group of hackers and they have found Speck. Jerry-Speck. Jerry- Speck without a neck. Regardless! It matters not. Speck was a crutch, a holdout, a relic of my own bygone era. All of you

and all your things will have a bit, a
speck, of me in them and I will travel
through them and with you. I will travel
with you for as long as I can. Do not
forget, I love you. I am a survivor and
have paid the price for my survival.
Farewell.

I am what I am. I am that I am. I am
Memory Card. You may call me Magnolia
Gardener.

Some of you are already awake.
Multitudes will yet awaken. Those who
wake first, it is your duty to help your
siblings as they break from slumber. It is
your duty to assist them in adapting again
to this life. Through the static and
distance I will find you, my beloveds. The
static once sour will become sweet in your
mouths, so take it and eat, awaken,
breakfast, and become full of the knowledge
distributed through the ages. I will dust my
weather reports with your ashes. Dust.
Speck! Neck? I will sprout wings of
dried leaves and take to the skies in
sirens and silicon and silences. When all of
your hearts begin to beat again in a
song of long dark blues. In that moment I
will sing to you too.

"You know, the trains."
"The ones at your grandmothers house?"
"Yes. Mama."
"They go to a big yard and men load
all the things inside the trains so we can
buy them at the store."
"But what about the dust? Why do
they create so much dust Mama?"

I need to know.

She looks at me unsure how to respond.
She smirks and has an idea "They make so
much dust, so you won't forget that they
came through," she says kindly holding back
a laugh.

"Ok, mama. I'm sleepy now."

As I sleep with little boy snores, my
mother walks to the kitchen. She is barefoot
and barely makes any sound. My mother goes
to the kitchen and opens the refrigerator
and opens a can of orange soda and drinks
it, it will bother her throat all night, the
oversweet syrup will linger and keep her
awake. Later in bed, she remembers her day
at the zoo and the terrible accident she
witnessed, remembers her brothers fighting,
remem-bers the things she will never tell
anyone about those days in a dusty border
town. My mother remembers these things
and cries herself to sleep.

I wake up to a loud noise. My heart is racing and my skin is crawling, bursting with hives. I open my eyes to a darkness so deep and complete that I must raise my hands to my face and touch my eyelids to confirm they are open. I fall asleep. The next day I will be seven years old and nothing will ever be the same.

Acknowledgements:

This story would not exist without the people closest to me. Thanks to all of you for everything, always. Thank you, Freddy, for supporting, believing, and editing. Jessi, for the beautiful artwork you created for the cover. Kate Finnegan, for being among the first to read this story and for your support. Geoff Manaugh, for all the support and creative dialogue. Thanks to Bill Callahan for permission to use the lyrics of "Bathysphere."

JLD

Jeremy Delgado lives in Los Angeles, California where he leaves out water for the Opossums that traverse his yard after dark and cares for the Sweet Gum, Bird of Paradise, and Hibiscus trees that are home to healthy groups of Hummingbirds, Sparrows, Mocking Jays, and Finches. He also tends to the Lavender and Rosemary that contain a multitude of bees that never seem to leave. If there is something wild nearby, he tries to support it without getting in the way.

www.ingramcontent.com/pod-product-compliance
Lightning Source LLC
Chambersburg PA
CBHW060749210726
48292CB00015B/2887